MISFITS ACADEMY
THE SUPER-SNEAKY SUBSTITUTE!

by Michael Anthony Steele
illustrated by M. Johnson

STONE ARCH BOOKS
a capstone imprint

Published by Stone Arch Books,
an imprint of Capstone
1710 Roe Crest Drive
North Mankato, Minnesota 56003
capstonepub.com

Copyright © 2025 by Capstone. All rights reserved.
No part of this publication may be reproduced in
whole or in part, or stored in a retrieval system, or
transmitted in any form or by any means, electronic,
mechanical, photocopying, recording, or otherwise,
without written permission of the publisher.

Library of Congress Cataloging-in-Publication Data
is available on the Library of Congress website.
ISBN: 9781669082408 (library binding)
ISBN: 9781669082361 (paperback)
ISBN: 9781669082378 (eBook PDF)

Summary: Niko and his friends have a funny
feeling about Mr. Reynolds. Not only is their new
substitute teacher asking students to use their
superpowers to test their safecracking skills, but
he also bears a striking resemblance to a criminal
kingpin! Is Mr. Reynolds really a supervillain in
disguise? And if so, how can Niko and his friends
foil the super-sneaky substitute's evil plans?

Designed by Kay Fraser

Any additional websites and resources referenced
in this book are not maintained, authorized, or
sponsored by Capstone. All product and company
names are trademarks™ or registered® trademarks
of their respective holders.

Printed and bound in the USA. 6121

TABLE OF CONTENTS

CHAPTER 1
LUCKY STREET 7

CHAPTER 2
WEIRD SCIENCE 13

CHAPTER 3
LOOK-ALIKE 19

CHAPTER 4
NEW DISCOVERY 24

CHAPTER 5
TEMPORARY HEADQUARTERS 31

CHAPTER 6
BAD WEATHER 36

CHAPTER 7
IN TROUBLE 42

CHAPTER 8
BIG REVEAL 48

CHAPTER 9
NO ONE LEFT BEHIND 54

CHAPTER 10
A SUPER TEAM 60

WELCOME TO MISFITS ACADEMY

THE SCHOOL

The Melissa Fitz Academy of Arts and Sciences was created for students gifted with superpowers that most people consider useless. Now nicknamed Misfits Academy, the school gives its students a safe space to blossom into their true selves.

THE MISFITS

NIKO
Nickname: Armor
Power: Can transform right arm into metal, but it is too heavy for him to hold up.

MONIQUE
Nickname: Slo-Mo
Power: Can tap into the Speed Dimension, but she only moves in slow motion.

MATEO
Nickname: Squall
Power: Can control the weather, but only two feet above his own head.

ELLIE
Nickname: Noodles
Power: Has magical abilities, but she can only make piping-hot chicken noodle soup appear.

AMIR
Nickname: Charger
Power: Can create electricity, but only enough to charge phones, tablets, or laptops.

CHAPTER 1
LUCKY STREET

"I like the academy and all," Niko said. "But I still don't see why I can't go to a regular school."

"We've been through this before," his father said as he drove. He glanced over at Niko in the passenger seat. "You're not a *regular* guy," his father added.

Niko shook his head and sighed. He didn't feel special. He glanced down at his right arm. Sure, he had a superpower . . . sort of.

"Look, son," his dad said. "The academy offers things regular schools don't. Besides, what about

Monique and the rest of your friends? You want to stay with them, don't you?"

Niko shrugged. "I guess so," he replied. He stared out the passenger window. He watched the houses zip by as they headed to school.

"And you'll grow into your power," Dad continued. "You'll see."

"That's what you and Mom keep saying," Niko muttered under his breath.

Niko's dad slowed the car as they turned a corner. The car sped up again. Police sirens blared in the distance. They grew louder.

"Looks like we just turned down Lucky Street," Dad said. It was one of his favorite corny sayings. Except this time, he meant it for real.

Ahead of them, three police cars chased a white van. They were heading right toward Niko and his dad. His father pulled over and opened his door.

"Another chance to see your old man in action," Dad said. He stepped out of the car.

Niko let out a long sigh. He had seen his father in action plenty of times. That's what it was like growing up with a famous superhero.

His father strolled toward the middle of the street. The police chase rocketed toward him. Niko's dad put his hands on his hips and began to change.

SHINK! SHINK-SHINK-SHINK-SHINK! SHINK!

Metal plates covered his entire body, head-to-toe. Niko's father was now the superhero, First Knight!

"Did you get any of your dad's powers?" the officer asked.

Niko squirmed in his seat. "Well . . . kind of . . ."

"You bet he did," First Knight said proudly. He marched over to Niko's side of the car. "Come on, son. Give me the super handshake," Dad said.

"Dad!" Niko whined.

"Just a quick one," Dad prodded. He reached his huge, armored hand into the car.

Niko shook his head. He reached up and took his father's hand. Niko concentrated and triggered his own superpower.

Shink-shink-shink! Shink!

Niko's right arm transformed. It grew almost as large as his dad's. The same metal plates covered it from his fingers all the way to his shoulder. First Knight shook the boy's hand. At least his dad was there to help him hold up his arm. Since Niko was so thin, his large metal arm was too heavy to lift.

"See," Dad said. "He's a chip off the old block!"

The police officer cocked her head. "So . . . just the arm, then?" she asked.

First Knight nodded. "For now. But he's growing into it."

Niko groaned with embarrassment.

CHAPTER 2
WEIRD SCIENCE

Niko's dad dropped him off in front of the school. Luckily, his father had transformed back to his normal self for the rest of the ride. Niko was relieved about that, at least.

Niko climbed the steps and passed under the main sign. Melissa Fitz Academy of Arts and Sciences. Of course, most of the students called it Misfits Academy. It was a school full of misfits, after all. All the kids had some kind of superpower—if you could call it that. Like Niko, they each had a special ability that hardly seemed helpful. Certainly not superhero material.

Niko swung by his locker and then headed to class. He took his usual seat in the back among his four friends.

"Now that we're all here," Amir said, "I can whip out some new names for our superhero group."

Monique chuckled. "Here we go again," she said.

"How about . . . The Chargers?" Amir asked.

Ellie rolled her eyes. "That's just your superhero name with an 's' at the end."

"Okay, okay," Amir said. "Then how about . . . Electro Force Five? Because there's five of us."

"Dude, you're the only one with electricity powers," Niko said. "And all you can do is charge cell phones."

Amir held up a finger. "For now."

"I can make lightning sometimes," Mateo admitted. He adjusted the rain hat on his head. "Except I usually just shock myself." Mateo wore his usual raincoat and hat. He could control the weather. But he could only create storms two feet above his head. Plus, he had trouble controlling his power sometimes. That's why he always wore rain gear.

A strange man entered the classroom. He had spiked blonde hair and wore thick-rimmed glasses.

"Hello, class," he said. "Ms. Jones is out sick today. So, I'm your substitute, Mr. Reynolds." He reached into his pocket and pulled out a strange metal object. "Let me just take roll." He set the device on the desk next to a list of the students signed up for the class. A tiny antenna rose from the machine and scanned the list with laser beams. Then the beams washed over the students. The device dinged.

"Ah, looks like everyone's here," Mr. Reynolds said.

Amir smiled at his friends. "Pretty cool," he whispered.

Mr. Reynolds clapped his hands together. "Science! One of my favorite subjects." He marched over to an object with a piece of cloth over it. "But today, we're going to do something a little different." He removed the cloth to reveal a small safe atop a rolling cart. He rolled the safe to the front of the class. "Who here has the power to open this safe?"

The students glanced at each other, confused.

"Any ideas?" Mr. Reynolds asked.

In the front of the class, a girl slowly raised her hand.

The teacher glanced at the roll book. "Zoey, right?" He waved her forward. "Step up and show us what you got."

Zoey slowly stood. "I can't open it, but I can get what's inside."

Mr. Reynolds's eyes widened. "Ooh, let's see!"

The entire exercise seemed strange. Their usual teacher just taught science basics. And sometimes Ms. Jones explained the science behind their powers.

Ellie raised her hand. "Mr. Reynolds? This seems more like a villain exercise, doesn't it? Breaking into a safe?" Several of the other students mumbled in agreement.

"Perhaps," the sub replied. "But what if some innocent victims were locked in a larger safe, hmm?"

"I guess so," Ellie said. The rest of the class seemed content with the answer.

Monique leaned over to Niko. "Doesn't this guy look familiar?" she whispered.

"How so?" Niko whispered back.

Monique snuck her phone out. She snapped a picture of the new teacher.

"I'm not sure," she replied.

CHAPTER 3
LOOK-ALIKE

Niko and his friends had their next class with Mrs. Lee. After she gave everyone their assignments, the students worked on their own. Monique was already busy on her computer.

Niko glanced at her screen. She had uploaded the photo of Mr. Reynolds from her phone. Monique pulled up another photo next to it. It was a man in a mug shot. Now he looked very familiar.

"This is what I'm talking about," Monique whispered. "Remember that supervillain our parents took down all the time?"

Like Niko, Mo had a parent in the Super Troupe superhero team. Her mother was Zoom, a speedster. That meant she could do anything at super speed.

Both Monique and Niko spent a lot of time at the Super Troupe Headquarters when they were little. They were quite familiar with most of their parents' missions.

"Oh, yeah," Niko replied. "Phineas Sharp. The guy that made all those weird gadgets and weapons. He tried to take over the world, like, a zillion times." Niko remembered him well. Sharp was one of the Super Troupe's biggest enemies.

Monique waved the others over. She showed them her computer screen.

"Hey, Amir," said Zoey. She held out her cell phone. "Do you mind?"

Amir let out a breath. "Sure," he said. He touched the cell phone. **ZZZT!** Small sparks burst from his fingertips. Zoey's phone was instantly fully charged.

Amir was very popular with the academy students. He could give their devices a full charge with a single touch.

"Thanks," Zoey said. She glanced up at the computer screen. "Is that Phineas Sharp? Kinda looks like that new substitute."

Monique's fingers raced over the keyboard. The screen went blank.

"We were just messing around," Monique explained.

"Hey, weren't you one of the kids he called on at the end of class?" Amir asked Zoey.

Niko had forgotten all about that. After the bell rang, the substitute listed a few names of students he wanted to speak with after class.

"Yeah," Zoey replied. "Mr. Reynolds is starting some kind of after-school club."

"What kind?" Ellie asked, leaning forward.

Zoey shook her head. "I don't know. I told him I'm in too many clubs already."

"You left before you found out what the club was about?" Monique asked.

Zoey nodded. "My parents would kill me if I joined another club." She returned to her workstation.

Niko glanced at the others. "Come on. What kind of club would a substitute start?" he asked.

A grin stretched across Amir's face. "A supervillain training club!"

CHAPTER 4
NEW DISCOVERY

Niko's next class was superhero history. Mateo was the only one of his friends who shared it with him. Niko didn't get to sit beside him though. Mateo sat in the back, just in case a small rainstorm formed over his head. So they didn't get to discuss Monique's theory about the substitute.

At lunch, after they had gotten their trays, the five friends sat at their usual table.

Amir leaned close. "So, have you heard—"

POF! Carter suddenly appeared beside their table. He could teleport, but only three feet at a time.

Amir jumped. "Man, don't do that!"

"Sorry," Carter said. "Ellie? Can I have—"

"Let me guess," Monique interrupted. "Some more of her world-famous soup."

Carter grinned. "I like it!"

"You bet," Ellie said. She held out her hand and closed her eyes. *PAF!* A cardboard cup of soup appeared.

Ellie was the daughter of the superhero Spellcaster. Like her father, Ellie had magic inside her. She could create things out of thin air—as long as that thing was a cup of hot chicken noodle soup.

"Thanks," Carter said.

"I wouldn't teleport with that," Ellie warned. "It's hot."

Carter nodded. "I know. Thanks again." He walked back to his table like a regular person.

"So, what were you saying?" Niko asked.

"The word is out," Amir said. "Everyone's talking about how we think Mr. Reynolds is a supervillain."

Niko winced. He was afraid of that. He didn't

know how it was in other schools. But rumors traveled fast at the Misfits Academy.

"Already?" Monique asked. She rolled her eyes. "Zoey and her big mouth."

Mateo wrung his hands. "What if Mr. Reynolds hears it?" he asked. "Are we going to get in trouble?"

Before anyone could answer, Theo and Enzo strolled up.

"All right, Niko," Theo said. "Let's go."

Theo was one of the biggest kids in school. He had the power of flight. But he didn't do it often. He could only fly backward, feetfirst. It was a cool power. He just didn't look very cool doing it.

Niko didn't think his power was good for much. But it was nice being able to beat Theo at arm wrestling.

Shink-shink-shink! His arm went back to normal.

"You think you're so tough," Theo said as he shot to his feet. He rubbed his sore hand. "But none of *you* are part of Mr. Reynolds's after-school project."

"Yeah," Enzo agreed.

"What project?" Ellie asked.

Theo shook his head. "Top secret. Invitation only."

"Yeah," Enzo added.

Theo bumped the table as they left. Monique's milk carton toppled over and fell off the edge of the table. Monique reached out to grab it and froze. At least, she seemed to freeze. She was actually moving in slow motion.

"Uh-oh," Mateo said. "There she goes again."

Like her mother, Monique could tap into the mysterious Speed Dimension. But she didn't move fast, like her superhero mom. Monique inched forward in slow motion whenever she tried to be fast.

The milk carton slowly emptied on the floor. Monique was still moving toward where it was when it began to fall.

"It's okay, Mo," Niko said. He tapped her on the shoulder. "It's too late."

Niko pulled his hand back. "Whoa."

"What is it?" Amir asked.

"I never noticed before," Niko replied. "But Monique is as hard as a rock when she's in slow motion."

The others reached over and felt her arm. Their eyes went wide.

Amir stood and pushed his hand in front of her outstretched hand. He strained as he pushed against it. Monique kept moving forward.

"She's unstoppable," Amir announced.

Monique snapped out of slow motion and glanced around. "I did it again, didn't I?" she asked.

"Yeah, but guess what?" Ellie asked. She explained what they learned. Everyone was extremely excited. A small rainstorm formed over Mateo's head. Soon, a puddle formed around him.

Mrs. Walsh, the janitor, had already walked up with a mop for the milk. She shook her head and handed it to Mateo.

CHAPTER 5
TEMPORARY HEADQUARTERS

While Mateo mopped up his mess, everyone finished their lunches and put away their trays. All the while, Amir couldn't stop talking about Monique's power.

"Maybe you're even bullet-proof, like First Knight," Amir suggested. "We should totally test it."

"What?" Ellie asked.

"I mean, we should start small," Amir admitted. His eyes widened. "I bet we could break a board on you!"

Monique rounded on him. "If you think you're hitting me with a board, you're crazy."

"I'm just saying, this is a great discovery," Amir said. "What a great addition to our super team!"

There he goes again, Niko thought. *Always going on about being a super team.*

Niko shook his head. "We're not a team," he said. "We're just some kids with weird powers." He led them out of the lunchroom.

Amir pointed to Monique. "Even after what we just learned?" he asked. "And we already have our first mystery." He held up both hands. "The Case of the Supervillain Substitute."

Ellie nudged and shushed him. "That rumor's already going around the school." She glanced around. "You want to make it worse?"

Niko spotted Theo and Enzo watching them from down the hallway.

Amir opened the door to the janitor's supply closet. "Quick, come in here."

"Really?" Monique asked.

Mateo cringed. "I don't like small spaces."

"Just for a minute," Amir said. He grabbed Mateo by the arm and pulled him in. The others reluctantly followed. Amir shut the door behind them.

"Okay, what's our next step?" Amir asked.

"Next step for what?" Niko asked. "We're not superheroes, and we're not a team."

Mateo glanced around nervously. "And this would be a really bad headquarters if we were."

Monique shrugged. "Well, if we were a team, and we were trying to solve a mystery . . . I guess we need to get proof."

Amir rubbed his hands together. "There you go!"

"Yeeee-ooow!" Enzo shouted from down the hallway. His stretched ear snapped back into the air vent.

Niko and his friends burst into laughter.

CLACK!

They stopped laughing. Someone had locked the closet door from the outside. They could hear Theo snickering on the other side.

Mateo pushed through the others. He tried to turn the knob, but it wouldn't budge.

They were trapped!

CHAPTER 6
BAD WEATHER

RINNNNNNNG!

The school bell blared in the hallway outside the closet.

"Great," Ellie said. "We're late for class. And I've never been tardy."

Amir smiled. "A small price to pay for being a superhero," he said. "I bet even Power Core was tardy sometimes."

Power Core was Amir's favorite superhero. He controlled electricity too. Except Power Core could do a lot more than just charge cell phones.

Mateo rattled the doorknob some more. It still wouldn't move.

"Oh, no, no, no . . . ," he said nervously.

Niko pointed to the dark cloud forming over Mateo's head. "I think that's the least of our problems."

Rummmmmble . . .

The faint sound of thunder filled the closet.

"It's okay, man," Amir told him. "We'll get out of here."

"Yeah," Niko agreed. "Mrs. Walsh was just in the cafeteria. I'm sure she'll be right over to get more supplies."

Mateo wasn't listening. "No, no, no . . . ," He kept trying the door.

RUMMMMMMBLE! The thunder grew louder.

KRACK! A small lightning bolt shot out of the cloud.

Everyone stepped away from Mateo. But they couldn't get very far in such a tight space.

"I don't think he's going to last that long," Ellie said.

Amir turned to Monique. "You can break the door down," he told her.

Monique shook her head. "What?"

"You're unstoppable, remember?" he said.

"I'm pretty sure that door is going to stop me!" Monique said.

KRACK! KRACK-KRACK!

More lightning appeared as Mateo panicked.

"I don't think we have a choice," Ellie said, dodging one of the bolts.

Monique sighed. "I'll try." She took a step back.

KRACK-KRACK!

"Better get closer," Niko suggested. "We don't have time for you to slo-mo all the way across the closet."

Monique nodded. "Right," she agreed. She moved closer to the door.

Niko ducked a bolt of lightning as he edged Mateo away from the door.

Monique raised her forearm and leaned forward. In slow motion, she moved toward the door. The lightning lessened as Mateo looked on, hopeful.

Monique finally reached the door. Then she snapped out of it. She shook her head. "It's no good," she said.

"Aw, man," Mateo muttered. More lightning shot from above his head.

"Maybe if you aim for a spot on the other side of the door?" Amir suggested.

"What? Really?" Monique asked.

Shink-shink-shink!

Niko's arm returned to normal. The smashed doorknob was still in his hand. It looked like an aluminum can someone had crushed to about half its size.

As everyone filed out of the closet, they stopped in their tracks. Mrs. Walsh stood in the hallway, staring at them. She glanced down at the junk in Niko's hand. Her lips tightened as she shook her head.

"Uh, whoops?" Niko said with a nervous laugh.

CHAPTER 7
IN TROUBLE

Niko and the others looked up as Monique exited the principal's office.

"What did she say?" Niko whispered.

Mrs. Payne shushed him. "I said, no talking," the secretary reminded them. Then she nodded at Niko. "You're next."

Niko got to his feet. He was the last of his friends to see Ms. Fitz. He timidly pushed open the door. The principal and founder of the academy stood beside her desk. She was short, barely taller than Niko. And much of her height came from her tall, poofy hairdo.

Ms. Fitz was usually lively and cheery. But today, she glared at Niko over the rims of her glasses.

"Take a seat, Nicholas," Ms. Fitz ordered. She was one of the few people who used his full name.

"I'm sorry about the doorknob," Niko said as he sat. "It's just that . . ."

Ms. Fitz held up a silencing hand. "I'm not thrilled about that," she said. "But that's not what I want to discuss. Did you hear the rumor about Mr. Reynolds?"

Niko winced. Of course he knew. He had helped start it—by accident.

"Well, we just thought . . . ," Niko began.

The principal silenced him with a slow shake of her head. "Oh, I've already heard about your theory from the others," she said. "You know rumors can be hurtful."

Niko sighed. "Yes, ma'am."

"Let me show you something," the principal said. She grabbed a tablet from her desk. She handed it to Niko and tapped the screen.

A video showed First Knight, his dad, bringing in a bad guy. The superhero marched a handcuffed criminal into the police station. The man was none other than the supervillain Phineas Sharp.

Niko handed the tablet back to the principal. "I've seen that before," he said. "My dad captures him all the time." He rolled his eyes. Of course, Sharp always escaped later. It was a classic supervillain move.

Ms. Fitz smiled. "You haven't seen this particular clip," she said. "That happened ten minutes ago."

Niko leaned forward in his chair. "What?"

"That blows your theory out of the water," she said. "Don't you think?"

"It sure does," Niko replied. He let out a sigh of relief. He wasn't completely onboard with Monique's suspicions.

"I told Mo," Niko said. "What would a supervillain want with a bunch of misfits—"

"Who attend *Misfits* Academy?" Ms. Fitz said, raising an eyebrow.

Niko's jaw dropped.

The principal chuckled. "Did you think I didn't know what the students called this place?"

Niko rubbed the back of his neck. "I . . . I don't know," he stammered.

Ms. Fitz waved him away. "Don't worry. I kind of like the name." She sat behind her desk. "You're not the only ones with so-called useless powers."

"That . . . that was amazing!" Niko said. The light faded. He removed the goggles.

Ms. Fitz put both pairs of goggles away. "You should never underestimate your powers," she said. "They may seem useless now. But they are part of what make you who you are. And you never know where they will take you."

"Yes, ma'am," he said. She had actually given him a lot to think about.

The principal stood. "Now, don't worry about the smashed doorknob," she said.

Niko let out a sigh of relief. He hadn't been looking forward to telling his dad about that one. Unfortunately, Ms. Fitz had a gleam in her eye. It didn't look as if they were getting off that easily.

"But I'm sure that rumor has gotten back to Mr. Reynolds by now," Ms. Fitz continued. "So, I want all of you to march down to his class this instant. He has a free period. And I think it's the perfect time to apologize for starting that rumor."

Niko nodded. "Yes, ma'am."

CHAPTER 8
BIG REVEAL

Niko led the way to Mr. Reynolds's classroom. He and his friends entered. They found the substitute alone at his desk. The sub held a screwdriver. He put the finishing touches on another homemade gadget.

"Mr. Reynolds?" Niko said. "We . . . uh . . . wanted to apologize."

"Apologize?" the sub asked. "Whatever for?"

Niko elbowed Monique. She stepped forward. "We kind of started a rumor about you."

"You did?" Mr. Reynolds asked. He didn't look up from his project.

Monique took a deep breath. "We . . . I thought you might've been someone else."

"We all did, sir," Ellie added.

Mateo rubbed his hands together nervously. A small dark cloud formed over his head.

"And who, pray tell, did you think I might be?" the sub asked. He still didn't look at them.

Amir laughed nervously. "You're never going to believe it," he said. "We thought you might be that big supervillain. You know? Phineas Sharp?"

Monique gave a nervous chuckle of her own. "Crazy, right?"

Mr. Reynolds snapped the cover shut on his gadget. It looked like a large remote control.

The substitute shook his head. "I really should work on my disguises." He pointed to the device on his desk. "I can create such amazing weapons. But I just don't have a knack for disguises."

Niko exchanged a puzzled glance with the others. "Excuse me?" he asked.

Mr. Reynolds stood. "I'm saying that, yes, I heard your silly rumor." He chuckled. "I'm also saying that it's not so silly after all."

The students looked at each other again.

The substitute gave a slow bow. "Phineas Sharp, at your service."

"I don't understand," Mateo said as a small drizzle splattered over him. The others inched away from him.

"Hello?" the sub asked. "I'm saying that you're right."

Niko shook his head. "But Phineas Sharp was just captured by my dad."

Mr. Reynolds gave a dismissive wave. "That was just one of my lackeys," he said. "He's an amazing shape-shifter. He handles all my big captures." The sub laughed. "After a while, he transforms into one of the prison guards and escapes."

Mr. Reynolds leaned closer and grinned. "Haven't you ever wondered how I always seem to escape from prison?"

Niko's eyes grew wide. He turned to the others. Their eyes were just as big. Could this guy really be Phineas Sharp?

"If you're really Sharp," Ellie said, "what are you doing here?"

"Why, looking for more lackeys," Sharp answered. "Most of you are useless, of course. But there are a couple that show some real promise."

Niko's lips tightened. Sure, he didn't think much of his superpower. But he didn't like this guy calling his friends useless.

"Why are you telling us this?" Niko asked.

"Oh, I got this one," Amir replied. "Bad guys like to brag about their big plans. Totally a supervillain thing."

Sharp nodded. "I'm afraid he's right," he said. "A bad habit, I suppose." He picked up the device from his desk. "Plus, I have this. One shot from one of my darts is all I need. You won't remember a thing." He aimed the weapon at Niko.

A dart shot from the weapon. Niko raised his arm to block it. His arm transformed. Then the weight dragged him down. Luckily, it pulled him clear of the dart. It sailed over his head.

"Look out!" Monique shouted. She tried to dash to one side. Instead, she went into slow motion.

CHAPTER 9
NO ONE LEFT BEHIND

Niko skidded to a stop. His friends nearly ran into him.

"What?" Ellie asked him.

Niko shook his head. "We can't leave Mo," he said. "We have to go back."

"Shouldn't we tell Ms. Fitz?" Ellie asked.

"Good idea," Niko said. "You guys do that. I'm going back."

"No way," said Amir. "We're a team. We should stick together."

Niko sighed. "Dude, we're not . . ."

A cloud rumbled over Mateo's head. "I agree."

"Me too," Ellie agreed. "We stick together."

Niko grunted in frustration. "Fine. Let's go!"

He led the way back down the hallway. Theo and Enzo were just stumbling to their feet. Cleaning supplies were everywhere.

"Ms. Walsh is not having a good day," Ellie said.

The kids made it back to the classroom. Phineas Sharp rummaged through a drawer. He pulled out a handful of darts and threw them on the desk. They slid everywhere as he began reloading his weapon.

Niko and the others crowded behind Monique. Luckily, she still moved in slow motion.

"Come on, Mo," Niko whispered. He tapped her stonelike shoulder. "Snap out of it."

Sharp shook his head. "Of all the ridiculous, brainless . . ."

Amir peeked out from behind Monique. "Hey! Who are you calling brainless?"

Sharp fumbled more with the weapon. "I'm calling myself brainless," he replied. "I should've never come here looking for lackeys."

"Lackeys?!" Theo asked. He and Enzo stood in the doorway. They were covered with blue cleaner and strips of toilet paper. "That's what your special club was all about?"

Sharp glanced up. "Of course," he replied. "Oh, and you're fired, by the way."

"We're no one's lackeys," Enzo said.

"Yeah," Theo agreed. "We're going to be superheroes someday!"

Sharp doubled over with laughter. He barely held on to his weapon. "Oh, please! A couple of misfits from Misfits Academy? With your useless powers?"

Mateo tapped Monique's shoulder. "She's not coming out of it," he whispered.

Niko glanced at the others. "Then let's show him some useless powers before he gets that thing reloaded," he said.

"Yeah," Amir said.

The four of them stepped out of their huddle. They stood in front of Monique.

Sharp had almost finished reloading. He looked up in surprise. "And just what are you misfits going to do?"

Niko nodded toward Sharp. "This guy looks a little hungry," he said. "Doesn't he, Ellie?"

Ellie smiled. "Oh, yeah," she said. A cup of chicken noodle soup appeared in her hand.

Phineas Sharp slid toward the open window. He hit the ledge and began to fall out.

Shink-shink-shink! Shink!

Niko's arm transformed. He dropped it onto the man's flailing legs. The weight of his mighty arm kept the villain from falling out—and from escaping.

"Let me go!" Sharp ordered. "Let me go!"

Just then, Monique snapped out of it. She walked up to the others. "What did I miss?"

"Not much," Niko replied. "Just a bunch of misfits capturing a real supervillain!"

Amir punched the air. "Yeah!"

CHAPTER 10
A SUPER TEAM

For the rest of the day, Niko and his friends were stars of the school. Even the next morning, students and teachers continued to congratulate them.

They didn't get much of a break during lunch. While they sat at their usual table, other students kept looking their way.

Niko was a little uncomfortable with all the attention. He wasn't the only one.

"When are people going to stop staring?" Mateo asked. A small cloud formed over his head.

Monique slid her lunch tray away from him. "Don't rain on my mac and cheese," she said.

"Besides, some new drama will soon get everyone's attention. It always does."

Niko nodded. "That's probably true," he agreed. There was always some daily buzz going around the school. He guessed it was like that for any school. But even more so in a school full of kids with strange superpowers.

Zoey swung by their table. She gave Amir a fist bump. "Good job, you guys," she said.

"All in a day's work for . . . Charge Force Five," Amir said with a wide grin.

Zoey cocked her head. "Who?" she asked.

Ellie rolled her eyes. "Don't listen to him," she said. "But thanks."

After Zoey left, Amir turned to the others. "We need a cool team name though."

"Yeah, but with an electricity theme?" Monique asked.

"We did make a great team," Ellie said. "But if it's named after anyone, it should be Niko."

Niko nearly choked on his sandwich. "Me?" he asked.

"Yeah," Ellie said. "You came up with most of the plans of attack."

Monique nodded. "She's got a point, man."

Niko shook his head. "They were just ideas. I don't know."

"You're a natural leader," Mateo added. "I couldn't have thought of all that."

"Yeah, but this team thing is Amir's idea," Niko said.

Amir raised both hands. "Hey, I agree with them," he said. "You totally led the way, dude."

Everyone nodded in agreement. Again, Niko didn't feel comfortable with the attention. But he had to admit that they took down Sharp like a real superhero team.

"How about I agree we make a great team?" Niko offered. "But just don't name it after me."

Amir nodded. "I'll keep working on a name," he

said. "But I already came up with cool superhero names for everyone. Want to hear them?"

Niko glanced at the others. "All right," he said. "Let's hear it."

Amir pointed at Mateo. "How about . . . Squall?"

Mateo giggled. "I like it," he said.

"Not bad," Monique added. "I'm surprised you didn't choose Lightning or some electrical thing."

Amir waved her away. "I'm past that." He pointed to Ellie. "Noodles!"

"Hey," Ellie said. "My mom calls me that!"

"You have to admit, it fits," Niko said.

Ellie shook her head. "Okay, for now. But I'm changing it if I can make something else appear."

"Deal," Amir agreed. He pointed to Monique. "I'm really proud of this one . . . Slo-Mo!"

Everyone laughed. "That's perfect," Ellie said.

"He's got you there, Mo," Niko added.

Even Monique chuckled. "All right. I'll allow it," she said.

Amir jutted a thumb at himself. "I'm Charger," he announced.

Everyone nodded. "We know," they said in unison. Amir had made no secret of his superhero name since they'd known him.

Niko winced as Amir pointed at him. "And for my man Niko," Amir said, "Armor!"

"Yes!" Mateo said. "That's great!"

"See, because you create this thick armor," Amir explained.

"I get it, dude," Niko said with a nod.

"And it's just on your *arm*," Amir continued.

Monique rolled her eyes. "We all get it."

Niko chuckled. "That's a good one though," he said.

Sure, Niko thought he had a boring superpower. But with the help of his friends, he saw just how much he could do with it.

"Hey, *Armor*," Theo said from behind him. "Ready for a rematch?"

Niko's shoulders slumped. *Not again*, he thought.

"Really, Theo?" Ellie asked. "You really want to embarrass yourself today?"

Theo shook his head. "Not with me," he said. He pointed at Monique. "With her!"

"What?" asked Monique.

Amir's eyes lit up. "That's perfect! Remember? I wanted to test the range of our powers."

Monique shrugged. "Okay," she said. She took another bite of her lunch. Then she sat down across from Niko.

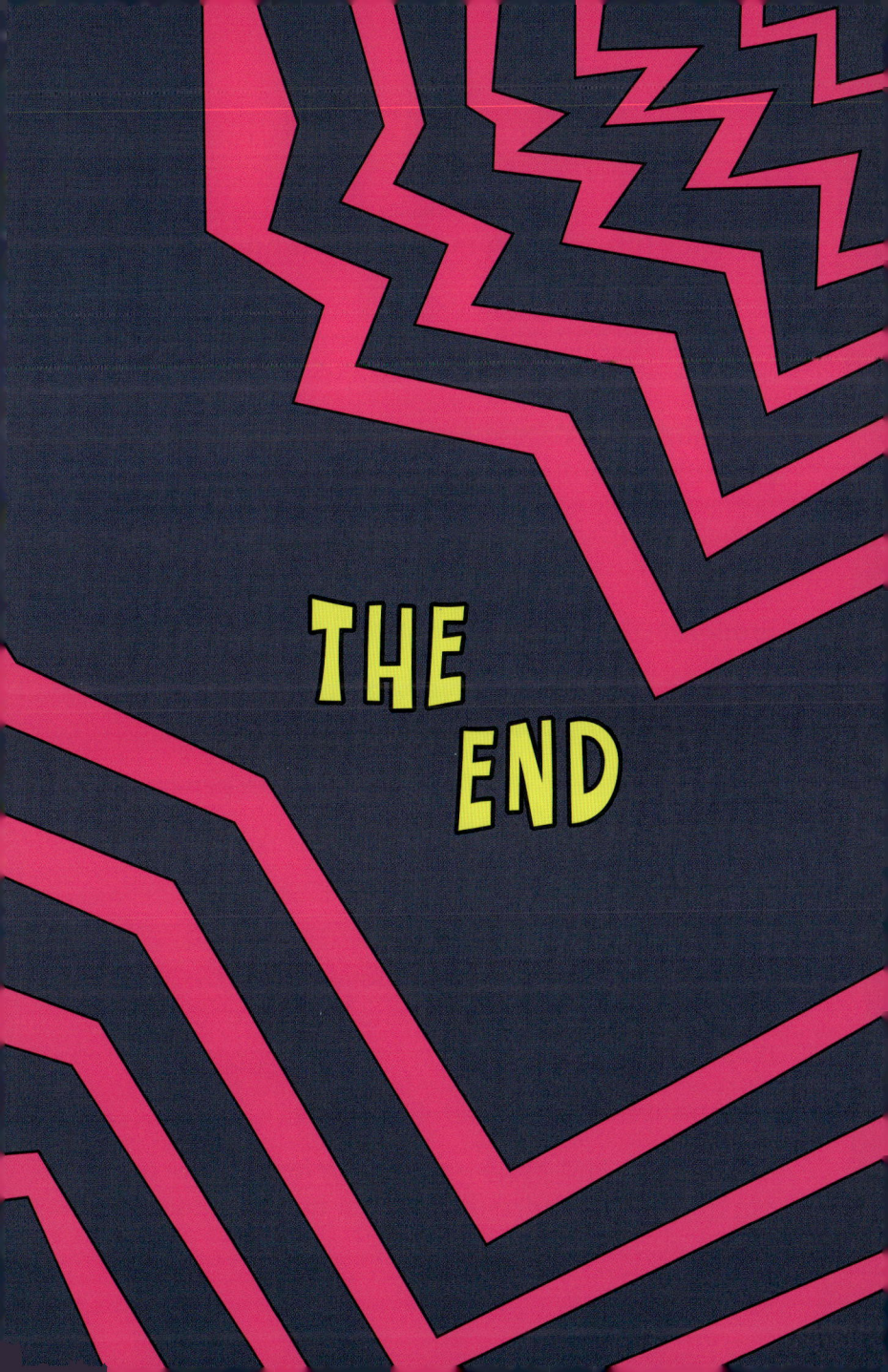

academy (uh-KAD-uh-mee)—a private junior high or high school

antenna (an-TEH-nuh)—a wire or dish that sends or receives radio waves

concentrate (KAHN-suhn-trayt)—to think clearly and put your full attention on something

dimension (duh-MEN-shuhn)—a place in space and time

innocent (IN-uh-suhnt)—not guilty

lackey (LAK-ee)—someone who does small tasks and errands for someone else

mug shot (MUHG SHOT)—a picture of a person's head taken at a police station

shape-shifter (SHAPE-SHIFT-uhr)—a person who can change form at will

teleport (TELL-uh-port)—to move oneself by instantly disappearing from one location and reappearing in another

transform (trans-FORM)—to change

tumbler (TUHM-blur)—an interior lever, latch, or pin that must be adjusted in order to open a lock

THINK ABOUT IT

1. Niko's dad is a superhero named First Knight. How do you think Niko feels about having a superhero as a parent? How would you feel if one of your parents had superpowers?

2. Ellie's superpower allows her to create chicken noodle soup out of thin air. If you had a power like hers, what kind of food would you like to be able to create again and again? Why?

3. Ms. Fitz says that with patience, students can find unexpected uses for their unique powers. What might be some unexpected uses for Niko, Ellie, Monique, Mateo, and Amir's powers?

WRITE ABOUT IT

1. Imagine you are a student at Misfits Academy. What would your unique superpower be? Write a paragraph explaining what your odd superpower allows you to do.

2. Monique's mom is a superhero speedster named Zoom. Write a short story about Zoom. Describe how she saves her city from an evil supervillain.

3. Phineas Sharp is known for escaping after he gets caught. Write another chapter for this book that explains what happens after he gets captured. Does he go to prison, or does he escape? You decide!

THE AUTHOR

Michael Anthony Steele has been in the entertainment industry for more than thirty years, writing for television, movies, and video games. He has authored more than 140 books for exciting characters and brands including Batman, Superman, Wonder Woman, Spider-Man, Shrek, and Scooby-Doo. Mr. Steele lives on a ranch in Texas, but he enjoys meeting readers when he visits schools and libraries all across the country! For more information, visit MichaelAnthonySteele.com.

THE ILLUSTRATOR

M. Johnson hails from the snowy mountains of the Balkan Peninsula where she grew up exploring the woods in the summer and stoking the fire in the winter. At an early age, she began escaping her small town by reading books about cursed kingdoms and different dimensions, chasing fantastical beings under bridges, and helping imaginary princesses save the realm. Today, Ms. Johnson lives in an airy warehouse in the heart of Worcester's Arboretum and adores illustrating strong female characters, colorful landscapes, magical adventures, and witty mysteries. Under her belt, she also has a BS in Film and Television Production as well as an MA in International Publishing.

JOIN MISFITS ACADEMY AND ENJOY ALL THE BOOKS IN THE SERIES

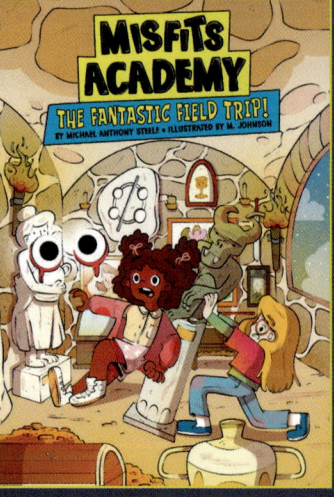
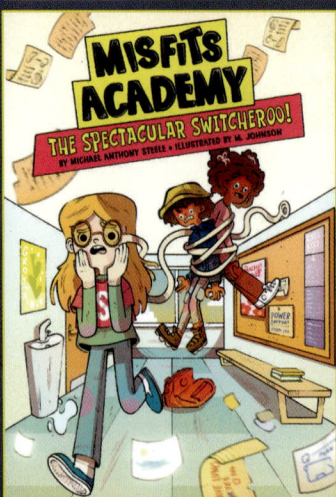
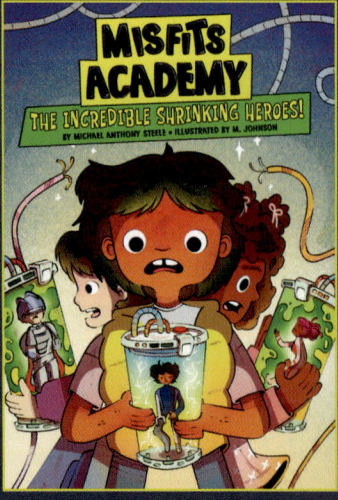